IN MY WORLD

written by JILLIAN MA

illustrated by MIMI CHAO

IN MY WORLD

All marketing and publishing rights guaranteed to and reserved by:

FUTURE HORIZONS INC.

721 W. Abram St. Arlington, TX 76013

Toll-free: 800·489·0727 | Fax: 817·277·2270

www.FHautism.com | info@FHautism.com

ISBN: 978-1-941765-43-2

Dedicated to all the people I love.
You are my perfect storybook.

— J.M.

Dedicated to those who long to be understood.

— M.C.

In my world,
I can adventure with my friend.

In my world,
my dreams have no end.

In my world,
I can dance
in the rain.

In my world,
I can fly
on a plane.

In my world,
I can sing with the birds.

In my world,
I can be seen and heard.

In my world,
I can race my toy cars.

In my world,
I can shoot for the stars.

In my world,
I can laugh and play chase.

In my world,
I can treasure every embrace.

In my world,
        I can play peekaboo
with a clown.

In my world,
I can hang
upside down.

In my world,
I can eat my
favorite snacks.

In my world,
I can share with
my friend Max.

In my world,
I can talk about
my favorite things.

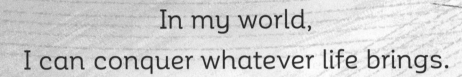

In my world,
I can conquer whatever life brings.

In my world,
I can climb mountains so high.

In my world,
I can fly free like a butterfly.

18

In my world,
I can smile like the
sun so bright.

In my world,
I can say
good morning

and good night.

In my world,
I can be calm and meditate.

In my world,
I can love and appreciate.

In your world,

I have Autism.

But with the help of you and you and you,

I can fulfill my dreams, and
make them come true.

Help me dream.

The Author

Jillian Ma is a Resource Teacher in British Columbia who has dedicated her life to working with special needs children. She obtained her Bachelor of Education degree in her hometown of Edmonton, Alberta. Prior to becoming a teacher, Jillian completed a Bachelor of Arts Degree with a double major in Psychology and Sociology. She was first exposed to working with special needs children as an educational assistant, and later became a Behavior Interventionist before turning her attention to education. Her students are some of the happiest, strongest, and most carefree people she has ever met, and they are her source of inspiration to write *In My World.* She truly believes that the meaning of happiness is having a kind soul and a loving heart. In her spare time, she likes to travel, create beautiful memories with her family and friends, and lend a helping hand to those in need.

The Artist

Mimi Chao grew up in the make believe worlds of *Calvin & Hobbes,* Studio Ghibli, and Roald Dahl ... and never quite grew out of them. Her work through her studio mimochai seeks to maintain that sense of wonder while integrating the perspective life brings. I*n My World* is Mimi's first published picture book. Having family members on the autistic spectrum, working on the book was a personally humbling experience. She is honored to have illustrated the message it shares. You can find more of Mimi's work at mimochai.com.

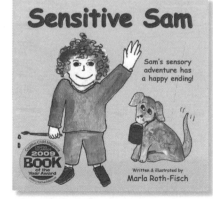